# Geraldine Pu

## and Her Cat Hat, Too!

### Written and illustrated by Maggie P. Chang

Ready-to-Read GRAPHICS

Simon Spotlight

New York    London    Toronto    Sydney    New Delhi

# For my brother

SIMON SPOTLIGHT

An imprint of Simon & Schuster Children's Publishing Division
1230 Avenue of the Americas, New York, New York 10020
This Simon Spotlight edition January 2022

For information about special discounts for bulk purchases, please contact
Simon & Schuster Special Sales at 1-866-506-1949 or business@simonandschuster.com.
Manufactured in the United States of America 1221 LAK
2 4 6 8 10 9 7 5 3 1
Library of Congress Cataloging-in-Publication Data
Names: Chang, Maggie P., author, illustrator.
Title: Geraldine Pu and her cat hat, too! / written and illustrated by Maggie P. Chang.
Description: Simon Spotlight edition. | New York : Simon Spotlight, 2022.
Series: Geraldine Pu | Summary: Geraldine Pu thinks her hair is boring and uses her cat
shaped hat to cover it, but after she tries to copy her grandmother's hair with disastrous
results, Geraldine learns to embrace her individuality.
Identifiers: LCCN 2021034225 (print) | LCCN 2021034226 (ebook)
ISBN 9781534484719 (paperback) | ISBN 9781534484726 (hardcover)
ISBN 9781534484733 (ebook)
Subjects: CYAC: Graphic novels. | Hats—Fiction. | Individuality—Fiction.
Self-acceptance—Fiction. | Hair—Fiction. | Taiwanese Americans—Fiction.
LCGFT: Graphic novels.
Classification: LCC PZ7.7.C419 Gd 2021 (print) | LCC PZ7.7.C419 (ebook) |
DDC 741.5/973—dc23
LC record available at https://lccn.loc.gov/2021034225
LC ebook record available at https://lccn.loc.gov/2021034226

# Contents

How to Read This Book . . . . . . . . . . 4

Words from Geraldine's World . . . . 6

Chapter One . . . . . . . . . . . . . . . . . . 7

Chapter Two . . . . . . . . . . . . . . . 20

Chapter Three . . . . . . . . . . . . . 34

Chapter Four . . . . . . . . . . . . . 48

A Message from Mao Maotz . . . . 62

How to Make a
Self-Portrait Collage . . . . . . . . 63

# How to Read This Book

This is Geraldine. She's here to give you some tips on reading this book.

It's me, Geraldine! The pointy end of this speech bubble shows that I'm speaking.

When someone is thinking, you'll see a bubbly cloud with little circles pointing to them.

This box I'm inside is called a panel. On each page, read the panels from left to right...

...and top to bottom.

Ta-da! Now you're READY TO READ this book!

GURGLE GURGLE

Oops, those gurgles were the sound of my tummy grumbling. It's time to eat!

HEE-HEE

# Words from Geraldine's World

Geraldine and her family speak English, Mandarin Chinese, and Taiwanese. Mandarin Chinese and Taiwanese are both languages spoken in Taiwan. Some of Geraldine's family members used to live there!

**Amah** (said like this: ah-MAH): the word for "Grandma" in Taiwanese.

**mao** (said like this: MOW, rhymes with "wow"): the word for "cat" in Mandarin Chinese.

**maotz** (said like this: MOW-tzz): the word for "hat" in Mandarin Chinese. Put "mao" and "maotz" together, and you get "cat hat."

**A note on the spellings in this book:**
There are different ways to write Mandarin Chinese and Taiwanese words in the English alphabet, but our book spells them the way Geraldine likes to spell them.

# Chapter One

Meet Geraldine Pu. Her last name rhymes with "two" and "moo."

Geraldine loves her family,

her favorite things,

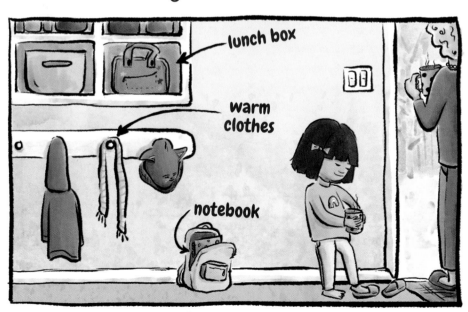

lunch box

warm clothes

notebook

and chilly weather. She adores getting comfy and cozy.

Mmm, hot cocoa!

One afternoon the wind makes Geraldine feel extra chilly.

But Geraldine smiles because...

...do you know what else she adores?

That's her cat hat. She calls her
Mao Maotz (said like this: mow MOW-tzz).

Her hat has darling ears and whiskers.

Best of all, I keep Geraldine's head warm!

Geraldine thinks her hat is...

15

That's Geraldine's brother, Auggie. Lately, he likes to copy everything she does.

Hey! I need my hat.

Amah said I can go with her to the hair salon, and it's cold out.

YOINK!

Auggie pouts.

At the salon the hairstylist compliments Geraldine.

18

So, Geraldine and Auggie find a place
to sit during Amah's haircut.

# Chapter Two

As they wait, Auggie pretends to be the hairstylist.

Meanwhile, Geraldine looks at photos of all kinds of hair.

She sees wavy hair like Amah's.

There's also hair that's

super short,

blond,

brown,

braided,

shaved,

and even spiky!

Geraldine thinks about how different and fun hair can be.

She wonders about her own.

It's straight.

It's black. And it's...

By then Amah's haircut is done.

WHISSH

It makes Geraldine smile.

Geraldine frowns, and it's not because Auggie's copying her.

The next day is chilly again, although the bus is quite warm.

Even then, Geraldine keeps Mao Maotz on.

She asks her friend Deven,

But Geraldine's still unsure about her hair.

Mao Maotz stays on Geraldine's head as
school starts...

...even though there's a strict rule:

NO HATS
IN SCHOOL

Nico notices right away.

Mr. Lunder, Geraldine's breaking the rules!

She tries to hide her whole head.

But she can still hear Mr. Lunder as he says,

As Geraldine returns to her seat, Mr. Lunder reminds the class,

# Chapter Three

When Geraldine gets home, she gathers supplies for her idea.

Once she's ready, she declares,

Then she brushes...

sprays...

wraps...

and squeezes gel...

all over her head.

When Geraldine tries to remove the curlers, she yelps,

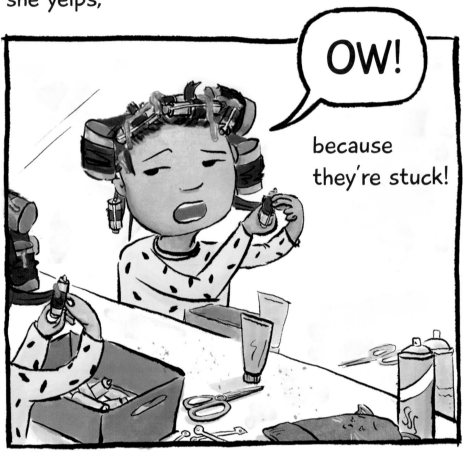

because they're stuck!

She mutters,

She picks up a pair of scissors, but before she can use them, she hears,

How am I going to get these out?

SNIP SNIP SNIP

Can you guess who's right behind her?

Geraldine turns to find her brother and...

...a chunk of his hair missing!

When Auggie sees himself, he starts to cry,

WAAAA!!!

40

Geraldine realizes Auggie wasn't the only copycat.

She was trying to copy Amah's hair for Picture Day.

Soon, they can't stop laughing at how silly they look.

47

# Chapter Four

Back at the salon, the hairstylists get to work.

BUZZZZZZ

BUZZZZZ

Before long, they're finished.

Looks great!

As they leave, Geraldine admits that she was trying to be like Amah.

Before she drives home, Amah tells them both,

Geraldine thinks about this and says to Auggie,

But Auggie's short hair makes him feel cold.

Suddenly, Geraldine shouts,

When she gets home
she gathers supplies
for her new project!

In the morning Geraldine lets Auggie borrow her hat again.

For her own head she has a brand-new, homemade...

...cat headband!

Geraldine explains,

My hair's not boring! Each day I get to ask myself: How do I want to style it?

Today...I want it like this!

SWISH

Yes! You get to keep your kitty style and rock a new hairdo, too!

Before leaving for school, Geraldine takes a peek in the mirror and says,

# The End

# A MESSAGE FROM MAO MAOTZ

People throughout the world are born with all different kinds of hair. It's great! In fact, sometimes people within the same family have different hair textures, like Geraldine and Amah do. Their hair is not the only thing that is different for Geraldine and Amah: When Amah was a child living in Taiwan in the 1960s, teachers wanted students to focus on studies instead of hairstyles. So, the school's rule was that every girl had to have the same short haircut. Because her classmates all had straight hair, Amah's wavy hair really stood out! Each year she would have to convince her teachers that her waves were natural. After some time, Amah learned to love her unique hair, and now she thinks her waves look great.

Throughout history, many hair trends have come and gone, but one thing has always stayed the same—people use their hair to express themselves! Similar to how your frowns and smiles can help others understand your feelings, what you do with your hair and what you wear on your head can be a way to share part of yourself. Your hair is yours, no matter what the color, how straight or curly, how long or short, and whether you have a lot of it or very little. So take care of it and have fun! And remember, expressing yourself is what style is all about!

What do you love about *your* hair?

# HOW TO MAKE A SELF-PORTRAIT COLLAGE

Another fun way people express themselves is through self-portraits. A self-portrait is art you make that is of yourself. There are many kinds of self-portraits, and this activity uses a mix of materials glued to paper to create a picture of your face. Art made from combining different materials is called a collage (said like this: kuh-LAHJ).

**Step 1.** Ask an adult to help you gather supplies:

- scissors
- glue
- mirror

- 2 pieces of paper: 1 for your background and 1 for notes

- collage materials of all different textures and colors like paper, cardboard, scraps of fabric, felt, yarn, ribbon, buttons, beads, gems, materials from the recycling bin, and everyday objects like small plastic spoons and straws. Anything that you are okay gluing down will do! You may even think of other materials to use when you're making your collage.

**Step 2.** Look in the mirror. What do you notice about your face? Ask a grown-up to help you write down what you see on a piece of paper.

**Step 3.** Use your notes from step 2 and your materials to make a self-portrait! First, use the other piece of blank paper as the background of your self-portrait. Then, start with your head. What material reminds you of this part of you? Cut out or arrange the shape you need and place it on your background paper.

For example, did you notice your head is round? If so, pick a material that has a color and texture that reminds you of your head and cut out a circle.

**Step 4.** Which part of your head or face would you like to add next? Your hair? Eyes? Nose? Keep going until you feel you've captured all the parts that make you you!

Tip: You can tell how people might be feeling by the way their mouths look. When you create your mouth for your collage, you can cut or arrange a shape to show how you are feeling—like a big, curved smile if you're feeling happy, or straight lips if you're feeling serious.

**Step 5.** Glue down all the materials you've arranged for your collage.

**Step 6.** Sign your art by writing your name on the paper.

**Step 7.** Ta-da! You have just made a self-portrait. Take a moment to admire your art!